My Snow Day
Ma journée de neige

Illustrated by Milena Radeva   Written by Ally Nathaniel

To my oldest son, Yuval, who can't wait for a sweet,
hot chocolate-milk on the first day of snow.

"What day is it today?" asked Gabi
as she sleepily opened her eyes.

❄ ❄ ❄

"Quel jour sommes-nous aujourd'hui ?",
demanda Gabi alors qu'elle
ouvrait ses yeux endormis.

"It's Saturday!" exclaimed her brother Adam.
"It's also a snow day!"
chimed in her sister Abigail.

❄ ❄ ❄

"C'est samedi !", s'écria son frère Adam.
"C'est aussi un jour de neige !",
ajouta sa sœur Abigail.

"It's time to get dressed
in our snow gear," said Gabi.

✳ ❄ ✳

"Il est temps d'enfiler notre
tenue d'hiver", dit Gabi.

They put on their snow pants, jackets, gloves, and hats. Then they put on their scarves and boots and rushed outside.

✳ ❄ ✳

Ils enfilèrent leurs pantalons de neige, anoraks, gants et bonnets.
Ils mirent ensuite leurs bottes et leur écharpe et se précipitèrent dehors.

"The snow is so clean and perfect!" remarked Abigail.

"La neige est tellement propre et parfaite !", remarqua Abigail.

"It's so bright and sparkly!" Gabi added.
"What should we do now?" asked Adam.
"Should we make snow angels?

❄ ❄ ❄

"Que c'est lumineux et brillant !",
ajouta Gabi. "Que pourrions-nous faire
maintenant ?", demanda Adam.
"Faire des anges dans la neige ?"

Should we make
footprints?

❋ ❋ ❋

Des empreintes de pas ?

“We should build
a snow-woman!”
answered Gabi.

“Nous devrions faire
un bonhomme de neige !”,
répondit Gabi.

They rolled the snow into three balls
and stacked them into a tower.
The big ball was on the bottom,
the medium ball was in the middle,
and the small ball was on top.

❄ ❄ ❄

Ils firent trois boules de neige
et les empilèrent pour former une tour.
La grosse boule était en bas, la moyenne
au milieu, et la petite au sommet.

"Let's go inside to get
some decorations!"
said Gabi.

❄ ❄ ❄

"Allons à l'intérieur
pour chercher
des décorations !", dit Gabi.

They found a carrot for the nose,
some strawberries for the mouth,
and two chocolate coins for the eyes.
They even found a colorful poncho
and a fancy hat.

* * *

Ils trouvèrent une carotte pour
le nez, des fraises pour la bouche
et deux pièces en chocolat pour les yeux.
Ils trouvèrent même un poncho
multicolore et un chapeau très chic.

Abigail created the face
and Gabi put on the hat.

❄ ❄ ❄

Abigail créa le visage
et Gabi mit le chapeau.

Adam wrapped it in the poncho.
The three of them proudly looked at their
beautiful snow-woman, and smiled.

❄ ❄ ❄

Adam l'enveloppa dans le poncho.
Tous les trois admirèrent
fièrement leur magnifique
bonhomme de neige et sourirent.

"Wow!" Their mom said,
"This snow-woman is perfect."

❄ ❄ ❄

"Ouah !" Leur maman s'exclama :
"Ce bonhomme de neige est parfait."

"You deserve a hot cup of sweet cocoa after all that work!"

"Yes please!"

"Vous méritez une tasse de chocolat chaud après tout ce travail !"

"Oui s'il te plait !"

Gabi took one last look at their
snow-woman and thought,
This has been the best snow day ever!

✳ ❄ ✳

Gabi regarda une dernière
fois son bonhomme de neige et pensa :
Ça a été le meilleur
jour de neige de ma vie !

Made in the USA
Monee, IL
09 July 2021